INSTEAD OF CHRISTMAS

Two Short Stories for December

With best wishes
for a merry Christmas
and a happy New Year
from

DEBBIE YOUNG

INSTEAD OF A CHRISTMAS CARD
Debbie Young

Copyright © Debbie Young 2015
All rights reserved
Published by Hawkesbury Press 2015
Hawkesbury Upton, Gloucestershire, UK
www.hawkesburypress.com

No part of this book may be reproduced in any form without the prior written permission of the author.
www.authordebbieyoung.com.

This book is a work of fiction.
Any resemblance to people living or dead
is purely coincidental.

ISBN 978-1519559104
Also available as two single story ebooks

CONTENTS

~ 1 ~
A Story for the Winter Solstice
Lighting Up Time

*First published as part of an online event
called Lighting Up the Darkness
organised by novelist Helen Hollick*

~ 21 ~
A Story for Christmas Eve
The Owl and the Turkey
or The Real Reason We Eat Turkey
at Christmas

*Previously published behind the door of a
Mumsnet online Advent Calendar*

LIGHTING UP TIME

A Short Story for the Winter Solstice

After hitting the loudspeaker button, I flung my mobile phone down on my desk. I hoped that physically distancing myself from my sister Kate's voice might stop me giving in to her, but I knew I was already a lost cause to her wheedling tones.

"I wouldn't have asked you to babysit if our usual girl hadn't come down with the lurgy, but you know the rule – no contact until 48 hours after you've thrown up. I can't risk sentencing the whole family to a sickly Christmas."

Kate's years of legal training had not been in vain. She can argue that black is white and people will believe her.

And so it was that I found myself driving out of town, down unlit country lanes, on the longest night. The winter solstice is the worst night of the year for anyone who, like me, is afraid of the dark.

Even if it had been broad daylight, I was still not ready to go back to Kate's, just six months after last summer's tragedy.

Well, ok, so it isn't really a tragedy when a 92-year-old woman dies. At work, I'm only allowed to use the word tragedy very sparingly when I'm writing up the obituaries. My editor would definitely blue-pencil it out in this case. But her death was traumatic for me, because I was the one who found her. And the 92-year-old woman in question was my lovely Great Aunt Sophie.

It was Midsummer's Eve and we were all out at Kate's country house to celebrate her husband Tom's 40th birthday.

Normally I'd consider it a treat to escape from the confines of my poky city-centre flat to soak up fancy food and drink at their expense. Tom's family own a posh car dealership, and what with Kate's salary as a lawyer as well, they are loaded. They'd pushed the boat out even further than usual this time, because they were also celebrating Kate's promotion to partner at her legal firm. It felt more like a wedding than a birthday bash, with me, as ever, like the bridesmaid, never the bride. But I'm not complaining. I could get used to Prosecco.

All the family were invited during the day, and friends and work colleagues were to join us for the evening. After games for all ages in the afternoon, there followed a buffet, then dancing to a live band in a marquee in the garden. The finale was a professional firework display, launched from the stable yard to give everyone a fine view from the vast terrace. It was a good thing there were no horses in the stables, only Tom's collection of classic cars.

Great Aunt Sophie was at the daytime celebrations, as she had been at every family party that I could remember. She'd even been at our house when I was born. I loved to hear her tell me of the first time she saw me, when I was just two minutes old. I had rosy pink cheeks, spiky fair hair, the loudest of cries and two big tears in the corners of my scrunched up little eyes.

From the day of my arrival, Great Aunt Sophie was so much a part of my life that I couldn't imagine ever being without her, even though I knew we'd have to part eventually. Whenever I'd been away from her for long, such as when I went off to university for three years, I'd keep a little bottle of her favourite floral perfume in my handbag. That way I could get a little hit of her summery aura whenever I missed her.

On that day last summer, she showed no sign of giving up the ghost, beating us all hollow at cards and charades. She was unimpressed by Tom's milestone birthday.

"Forty? That's nothing! I'm in my 93rd year, I'll have you know! That's you twice over, young Tom, plus Zoe and Archie too."

Zoe and Archie are Tom and Kate's kids, aged ten and three.

Zoe had recently mastered her times tables.

"So you're nine times me plus one Archie," she pronounced. "No wonder you get so tired."

Sure enough, Great Aunt Sophie was flagging by the time the evening guests arrived. She pottered off contentedly to bed around 8pm, shrugging off sympathetic looks as she made herself her usual bedtime mug of cocoa.

"I'll have the last laugh on you, my dears. I'll be fresh as a daisy at dawn while you're all nursing sore heads."

I chinked my Prosecco glass against her mug, suspecting from my already spinning head that she'd be right.

Next day I woke up at 8.47am, according to the clock that was ticking too loudly on the table beside my bed in

Kate's guest room. Trying to remember exactly when and how I had got to bed, I staggered to the door. I kicked out my way the clothes I'd apparently discarded on the bedside rug the night before and headed off on a quest for orange juice, my hangover remedy of choice. As I stepped out onto the landing, I had to squint against the sun that was streaming down through the stained glass window over the stairs, scattering coloured shadows across the pale parquet floor. I had to turn my head away from its glare. I caught sight at the far end of the corridor of a white heap, crumpled at the foot of the full-length mirror on the wall. Oh God, I thought, someone's been sick in the night and dumped their sheets on the landing for Kate to wash – charming!

When my eyes adjusted to the shadows, I realised that it wasn't a soiled sheet but a pristine cotton nightdress, containing the frail body of my Great Aunt Sophie. I ran to help her up, but even before I'd knelt down beside her, I realised that it was too late.

Gently I stroked the papery skin on the back of her hand, as familiar as the taut flesh on my own. Though her hand still exuded the perfume of her favourite hand-cream, night-scented stock, its raised veins were still.

Only when I saw Tom reflected in the mirror, framed in the doorway of his and Kate's room behind us, did I realise that I had screamed out loud. Tom staggered across the landing to stand over us both, hands in his dressing gown pockets.

"Christ, she looks how I feel!" he began. "I thought Sophie was sticking to cocoa, but maybe she was the one who drained that litre bottle of sherry."

Kate hurried out from her bedroom to find out what all the fuss was about, hastily tying the belt of her silk kimono.

"Tom, you moron, Sophie's not drunk, she's bloody dead!"

Tom's face turned ashen. He must be mortified, I thought – no that's the wrong word, replace it with gutted.

A more appropriate choice of vocabulary, it turned out, because straight away Tom dashed to the bathroom to be noisily, violently sick. Kate, meanwhile, all efficiency as ever, grabbed the nearest phone and took charge of the situation. Before lunchtime, a discreet black van marked "private ambulance" had swept up the drive and away again, taking Great Aunt Sophie with them. I never saw her again.

The post-mortem decreed she had died of natural causes, and after the funeral, life carried on for us all, except for Great Aunt Sophie. The only difference for me, apart from her excruciating absence, was that I began to find excuses to avoid going back to Kate's house. I couldn't bear to see again the place where my beloved aunt had died. Until tonight, I thought Kate had understood. She had at least been letting me off the hook.

I knew I'd have to go there some time, but not for something as trivial as babysitting. I tried to engage my objective journalistic judgement. I was being foolish. I was letting the inevitable death of one very old lady cut me off from the rest of my family. I had to snap out of it. But why tonight of all nights? The longest, darkest night, which I usually spend at home, with my flat lit up like a Christmas tree and with something jolly on the telly.

I don't know why the dark upsets me so, but I can't remember a time when it didn't. I always slept with a nightlight in my childhood bedroom, a much brighter one after Kate had moved into her own room when she was about twelve. I even took a nightlight away with me to university.

For someone on a tight budget, I spend a ridiculous amount of money on electricity in winter, just so that I can keep lots of lights on. One of my friends, an environmental campaigner, only ever lights up the room she is actually in. If I had to do that in the winter, I think I'd die. Either that, or move to a bedsit, so I had only one room to worry about.

Even keeping all the lights on is not enough for me. Although the power never goes off in the city, I keep a wind-up torch and candles in every room, in a place where I know I can put my hand on them, just in case we're ever plunged unexpectedly into the dark. I take comfort from the fact that from my tiny top floor balcony, I can see lights twinkling all over the city.

In a former life I must have been a swallow. I'd love to be able to fly south as soon as the nights draw in. I'd only return when the nights were no longer than the time I need to sleep.

What would happen if I had to spend time in the dark? I don't know, because I've never had the courage to find out.

When I got to Kate and Tom's, my heart was pounding. I forget just how dark the countryside is until I get to the point beyond streetlights. I always drive the last three miles with the map-reading light on in my car. I don't know how people live out in the sticks, with only the moon and stars to brighten the night.

I pulled my car up as close as I could get it to Kate's front door. Thankfully, their security light came on just after I swung the car door open. My foot crunched down on the gravel, sounding for all the world as if I'd stepped on a pile of light bulbs, and I let out a shriek.

As Kate led me through to their living room, I could tell from the extravagant array of snacks on the coffee table that she had been feeling guilty about dragging me out on such a dark night. Olives, pistachios, kettle chips, and Belgian chocolates lay alongside a newly-opened bottle of Rioja and a single, large wine glass – the sort they give you in pubs that nestle comfortably in your hand but make you drink much more than you intend. She knows Rioja is my absolute favourite, even better than Prosecco in the winter.

"I can't drink that, I've got to drive home later," I objected, already worrying that the lanes would be even darker after midnight.

"Don't be stupid," said Kate. "You must stay the night. I've got the guest room ready for you."

I thought it better not to tell her that I wasn't prepared to go upstairs, even though that's where the children's bedrooms were. What kind of babysitter was I?

Kate chucked a couple more logs on the crackling fire before tipping about a third of the bottle into the glass on the coffee table. I glanced around the room, scanning for candles. I knew that power cuts were frequent in this old house on windy nights. I spotted three fancy scented ones with multiple wicks in glass jars, the sort that cost as much as a standard lamp. I felt in my pocket to check for the matches and tiny torch that I always carry on winter nights.

"We've got a taxi booked for half past midnight, so we'll see you about one," said Kate, wrapping a crimson pashmina about her shoulders. "Feel free to go to bed before we get back if you want to."

I scowled. There was no way I was going upstairs to bed, past all those shadows and dark corners, with no light switch within reach before you were halfway down the landing. I grabbed the Sky remote, ready to distract myself the minute Kate and Tom had gone.

A moment later, a slight figure appeared in the living room doorway.

"Hello, Emma," said Zoe. She had recently dropped the Auntie title on the basis that she's nearly a teenager. (Nearly? She's 10 – she must be as bad at maths as Kate.) Not having seen her for a few months, I was for a moment startled by how similar she is to Kate – same long-lashed green eyes, same fine dark hair, falling in shiny waves to her shoulders, which, just like Kate, she shrugs in a particular lopsided way when she's restless or bored. In fact, I always think of Kate as being about ten, which was about how old she was when I first became aware of ages. I'd have been five. Archie is much more like me, with straight lighter hair, blue eyes, and a serious look. Sometimes, when we're all out together, which has happened less often lately, people will assume he's mine and only Zoe belongs to Kate. It's funny how genes sometimes side-step through family trees, taking with them distinctive mannerisms and ways of speaking as well as looks and personality.

"Archie's in bed already, because he's been a bit zonked since having his latest cold ," Zoe was saying. "I'm off to bed too now, night night."

She came over to give me and her mum a kiss.

"Please will you tuck me in before you go out, Mum?"

So much for the nearly-teenager.

I awoke, shivering on the sofa, just after the ten o'clock news had finished. The log fire had dwindled to ash, dotted with orange sparks. Hauling myself up from the sofa, I shuffled across to throw a handful of kindling on to the sparks, followed by a couple of logs. They weighed much less than I expected, then I realised they'd have been stacked in the stables drying since the spring. What luxury to have so much space. The fire quickly revived and was soon crackling like gunshot in the grate. I jumped at every tiny explosion.

Turning my stiff back to the fire to warm it, I remembered that I still hadn't adjusted my office chair as I'd been meaning to. Always too engrossed in bashing out my latest news story on the keyboard, I never remembered to adopt the health-and-safety-approved posture until my back ached.

It was only while surveying the room with a rapidly warming bottom, like some lordly Victorian gentleman, that I remembered that Kate and Tom didn't bother with curtains in their house. Facing me on every wall was a large, blank window, giving a view of nothing but the blackest of nights. Wherever I turned, I could see a window. And I really didn't want to look.

Ever since we read Henry James' *The Turn of the Screw* at school, when I was about 14, I've had a thing about curtainless windows at night. The book includes terrifying scenes in which two servants, dismissed in disgrace, come back to press their face against the glass after dark, sinister with some unspoken threat. I cannot think of anything more frightening – the cold, dark threat of the unknown, emerging from the depths of one's own imagination. I'm not even sure now whether I've misremembered it, but I daren't go back and re-read the book to check, in case it makes it worse rather than better.

I cupped my hands around my eyes, attempting to create the effect of a horse's blinkers, and concentrated on the telly, my pulse loud in my ears. Rummaging in my pocket for my matches, I stooped down to light an exotic-looking, five-wicked candle beside the fireplace. I didn't care how much it must have cost Kate, I just needed all the light that I could get.

I tried to fool my brain into thinking I was relaxed by slumping back on the sofa and breathing slowly and deeply. The sound of my pulse was just receding when I heard the creaking of a door. With a shriek, I looked around, then realised with relief that it had come from upstairs. It was probably Zoe going to the loo or getting a glass of water, rather than a burglar or a ghost. I tried to attend to the panel game that was just starting up on Channel 4, ignoring the glass of Rioja tempting me to take some Dutch courage. I heard the door creak again as Zoe pattered back across the parqueted landing to her room.

Then just before the start of Round 3, a noisy coughing started upstairs. I shifted uncomfortably in my seat, hoping it would quickly abate. It sounded shrill - definitely Archie rather than Zoe.

Zoe will sort him out, I told myself, hopefully. She doesn't need me to go upstairs. I'm not going upstairs. I'm staying by this bright and cosy fire.

Archie continued to cough.

The jasmine-scented candle was starting to weave its way down into my lungs and made me give a little cough of my own. Feeling my chest tighten brought me to my senses. Kate is my sister, I suddenly thought, and she's a lawyer too. I can't let her son die of neglect, just because I'm too afraid to go upstairs.

On impulse, I knocked back half the glass of Rioja, hoping there was still time for it to wear off before I had to drive home. Then I seized the pale shawl that lay artistically draped across the rocking chair and wrapped it tightly around my shoulders, like symbolic armour against the dark on the stairs. Cautiously I crossed the hall to the foot of the dark oak stairs and began to climb them carefully.

Please stop coughing, please stop coughing, I urged Archie at every tread. Don't make me come all the way up. I proceeded as quietly as I could, as if silence might reduce the danger lurking in the shadows.

Archie went on coughing as I rounded the dogleg half-landing. The higher I went, the darker it was. The only source of light was a tiny glimmer of moonlight through the stained glass window above the stairs. I couldn't believe Kate hadn't left the landing light on. Wasn't it dangerous to have unlit stairs? It wasn't as if she couldn't afford the bill.

Archie's coughing was becoming shriller, tighter, grating on my nerves.

At least he's breathing, I comforted myself. No real harm done yet. But what was Zoe thinking? Why wasn't she in there helping her poor little brother?

Finally I reached the top of the stairs and turned left towards the children's bedrooms. Then I stood stock still, for there, at the far end, who should I see but my aunt, standing in the spot where she had died? Great Aunt Sophie, shrouded in white, was staring back at me, her long pale hair adrift from her habitual bun and streaming down her shoulders, thicker and lusher than I'd ever seen it in her life.

Who was it that said "Death becomes her?"

I didn't know I'd screamed until Zoe flung open her bedroom door, flicking on the hall light switch and casting a full hundred watts upon me and on Great Aunt Sophie. Except it wasn't Great Aunt Sophie at all, but me, like a frightened deer caught in car headlights, staring at myself in the mirror.

That was when I realised Archie had stopped coughing.

Tearing into his room, with Zoe right behind me, I snapped on the light switch on the wall (no nightlights in this house, cruel mother that Kate is) and dropped to my knees at the side of his tiny bed. It's the sort that you pull out to make it bigger every time your child grows. It reminded me of a child-sized coffin. Archie's eyes were closed, cheeks pale, body still, and sticking out of his mouth was a small plastic toy zebra. I grabbed it quickly and flung it across the room, seized him by the shoulders and shook him.

"Archie, Archie, breathe, for God's sake!"

After what seemed like hours, he stirred slightly, took a noisy deep gasp, puffed it back out, and resumed his usual steady breathing, tinged with a snuffly baby snore.

As I lay him gently back down on his side, hoping I hadn't dislocated any bones, he didn't even open his eyes. He just settled straight back down to the easy sleep of a small child.

Zoe, meanwhile, calmly collected the toy zebra from the other side of the room, gave it a token wipe on her nightie, and stood it up neatly beside its twin on the gangplank of Archie's toy ark.

"I don't know why you're making such a drama out of it, Emma," said Zoe. "Anyone would think you were scared of the dark."

I emitted a false little laugh and hoped it fooled her.

"Haha. Back to bed now, Zoe, or your mum will be cross with you."

"No, she'll be cross with you, Auntie Emma," replied Zoe firmly and trotted obediently back to bed.

After making sure there were no other choking hazards within Archie's reach, I pulled his door nearly closed but not quite, just to be on the safe side, and turned back to stare at myself in the mirror. With Kate's pale wrap around me and with the shadows cast across my face by the moonlight, I really did look a lot like Great Aunt Sophie. As I stood there smiling at my reflection, I felt comforted. Maybe she wasn't as far away as I had thought.

Pottering slowly back down the stairs, I began to wonder what my children would look like, if I ever get round to having any. Would they get any of Sophie's genes, or would they turn out like Kate? Or Mum? Or Dad? Or me? I supposed I'd just have to wait and see.

I'd finished the Rioja by the time Kate and Tom got home, and I was busy writing in the shorthand pad that I always keep in my satchel. I was making a list of the scented plants that I'm going to put in my window boxes this spring: narcissus, wallflowers, hyacinths, and of course Great Aunt Sophie's favourite night-scented stock. I'm looking forward to sitting on my balcony when the days are at their longest, a glass of something cool and refreshing in my hand, looking out across the cityscape rooftops and breathing in the perfumes of the flowers of the long summer nights.

Kate thought I didn't notice her fall off her designer heels as she got out of the car on the drive, but I'd been watching them through the big front window in the lounge.

"Kate, have you ever noticed how much I look like Great Aunt Sophie?" I asked her casually, as she took off her shoes and flung her crimson pashmina over the back of the rocking chair.

She gave me that knowing look that only big sisters can pull off.

"Of course you bloody do, have you only just noticed? Now get to bed, you look knackered."

"Okay."

I heaved myself up from my comfortable wallowing position on Kate's soft leather sofa and gave her a goodnight kiss, though not so light that it didn't leave a little Rioja stain on her cheek.

"Thanks for having me," I said, unnecessarily, before making my way up to the guest room, not forgetting on the way past the mirror on the landing to give Great Aunt Sophie a little wave.

The End

THE OWL & THE TURKEY

or

The Real Reason We Eat Turkey at Christmas

Foreword

When my daughter was eight years old, she announced just before Christmas that she was turning vegetarian. Next morning, as I pottered around the kitchen debating whether to bother cooking a traditional Christmas dinner when there were now only two carnivores in the house, I caught a snippet of news on the radio that seemed to have immediate relevance to my dilemma. According to BBC Radio 4's Today programme: "The problem is that Turkey does not have its own defence missile system."

It was a few moments before I realised that this wasn't a "silly season" story about festive catering options, but a serious report about conflict in the Middle East. But it was too late to prevent the following story unfolding in my imagination.

It was the afternoon of Christmas Eve, and the newly-crowned Queen was not looking forward to the next day's festive banquet. Not roast boar again! She drummed her fingers impatiently on the wooden embroidery hoop that lay neglected on her lap.

For generations, roast wild boar had been the focal point of the royal court's traditional Christmas feast. But the new Queen's sensitive young palate was bored of roast boar. And of deer and elk and moose, for that matter. She was not impressed by any of those cumbersome creatures that the huntsmen insisted on dragging in for her dinner. Why had her late father, the King, like all men, always thought that the biggest catch was the best?

Well, she was Queen now, and if she wanted a more elegant centre-piece for the royal festive table, then a more elegant one she would have. She called to the servant that stood to attention by the door, always poised to rush off on any errand that took her fancy.

"Thomas, please summon the royal huntsmen," she commanded. "And be quick about it. It will be dark in a couple of hours, and I need to dispatch them without delay."

While awaiting the huntsmen's arrival, she distractedly added a few stem stitches to her embroidery.

The golden thread rasped against her palm as she pulled the fine bone needle through the taut linen.

Suddenly there was a commotion at the door. A dozen huntsmen, dressed for action with knives in their belts and crossbows slung over their shoulders, were jostling against each other on the threshold. Each wanted to be the first to present himself to the Queen. She disregarded their open rivalry; she did not care for such obvious showing off.

"My huntsmen, I command you to go out into the forest straight away, and in the remains of the daylight catch something different for tomorrow's Christmas feast," she instructed them. "Something small that can be baked in the bread oven. Nothing huge that needs roasting for hours on a spit, looking for all the world like it's being tortured. If I want to watch torture, I'll do so in the dungeons, not the dining hall. I want faster food. Bring me a lighter, more compact creature than the usual wild boar – something that may be served up straight from the kitchen to the table. It has to look pretty, too."

The huntsmen exchanged anxious glances. It was an unusual request, but they dare not refuse a royal commission. On this late December afternoon, they'd have to work fast if they were to accomplish their mission before dark.

"I'll give ten guineas to the huntsman who provides the best creature," she added, rather hoping the victor would be young and handsome.

The huntsmen perked up at this offer and immediately set off from the royal castle. Some headed for the hills, others down to the sea, but the two youngest and best-looking, Piers and Giles, decided to stay closer to the castle.

Off they stalked into the thick, dark woodland that lay immediately beyond the moated walls. Ignoring the tell-tale tracks of big game on the ground before them, they headed purposefully towards the lake where they knew smaller animals went to drink. As they entered the lakeside clearing, they heard the sound of strong wings beating above their heads.

"Birds! Of course, we should stalk birds!" cried Piers, watching a plump grey goose rising into the steely sky where no sun shone. "Light to carry, quick to cook, and unspeakably pretty to serve, especially if you retain some fancy feathers for decoration."

From the top of a nearby elm, a rook with an inflated idea of its own good looks immediately took flight, loudly cawing its disapproval of their scheme.

"Plenty of them around, too," said Giles, wondering how much flesh there would be on a rook. "It's just a question of catching them."

Their hunter's instinct bade them to fall silent as they trod softly onward along the path that led to the lake. As they approached the water's edge, they could already see five swans idly drifting by, ignorant of the huntsmen's intentions.

"So shall we go for a swan, then?" whispered Piers. "You don't get birds more elegant than swans. They're beautiful."

Giles narrowed his eyes against a shaft of winter sunshine that was just breaking through the clouds. He stared thoughtfully at the plumpest swan.

"Imagine it dead, though. That long, elegant neck would flop about like a string of sausages. Not exactly pretty on the plate."

"Ducks, then," said Piers, turning his gaze to a newly-landed mallard. The glossy bird was waddling contentedly along the shoreline, teal flashes glinting on its folded wings, droplets of water rolling proverbially off its back. "A duck's just a swan on a smaller scale, but without that overstated neck."

He took a few cautious steps towards the mallard, but was stopped in his tracks by a loud squelch. Looking down to the source of the disgusting sound, he realised his nut-brown calfskin boot was now caked in dark green sludge.

"Ugh! Duck droppings! Disgusting! I'm not carrying one of those back to the palace. It would wreck my tights."

The duck emitted a mocking quack and relaunched itself onto the lake before its pursuers could change their minds. Forlorn, the two huntsmen sat down on a fallen tree trunk to reconsider. As they stared hopelessly at the lake, the water stirred gently beneath the chill December breeze. A few skeletal leaves skittered around their feet.

"If swans and ducks won't do, the only alternative out there is geese, and surely they're the worst of both worlds – the unwieldy long neck of a swan, but the grubby looking feathers of a duck," said Giles, watching the departing mallard carve a v-shaped trail across the lake's silvery surface. "I'm not sure this was the best place to come after all."

"Bigger poo, too, from a goose," agreed Piers. "So how about a peacock? You can't say a peacock wouldn't look pretty on a plate."

"Oh yes, I can!" retorted Giles. "It's all very well when they're wandering about the palace gardens, preening themselves and displaying their tail feathers, but imagine the difference when they're roasted. Their fancy tails would lie flat, trailing off the edge of the platter not standing up like a fan, and you'd barely see their fancy colours. Weird little heads they've got, too. Not nice. Not a pretty sight at all."

Slouching forward, Piers passed his hand across his face as if to clear his thoughts. Suddenly he sat bolt upright, inspired.

"What's the Queen's favourite colour?" he asked. "Maybe there's a clue in that. Something really bright and cheerful would be festive. Red? Or blue or yellow?"

A small blue tit that had been watching them from its perch on a low-hanging branch didn't wait around to hear the answer, and a nearby red squirrel lobbed an acorn at the huntsmen in angry protest.

Giles shook his head, gazing blankly into the distance. "Maria says the Queen loves white at the moment," he said with the allowable authority of a man courting the Queen's wardrobe mistress. "Pearls, ivory, diamonds – the less colour the better. It's the latest fashion from Vienna, apparently, more flattering for pale skin. So anything highly coloured won't be well received."

Piers pointed to a small stone cottage perched beside the lake a few hundred yards away.

"Let's go and see the royal eggkeeper," he suggested. "Maybe he'll let us have one of those fancy big white birds that the royal explorers just brought back from foreign parts. I hear they've not been very productive on the egg front. Everyone's still eating hens' eggs."

"I hear those new birds are fat and stupid, and don't fly much," said Giles. "They should be easy enough to catch. I wonder what they taste like. They must have some redeeming features."

Piers shrugged. "There's one way to find out."

Feeling more cheerful, they got up and headed for the royal eggkeeper's cottage. Entering the old man's walled garden, they disregarded the tawny coloured chickens scratching about in the undergrowth. Instead they set their sights on the chickens' bigger, more exotic cousins. Although these so-called turkeys (that were, court rumour had it, not from Turkey at all) had settled comfortably into their new home alongside the native flock, their size made them easy to spot. With snow-white feathers, these portly creatures were certainly of a colour that Her Majesty would find acceptable. Their otherwise neat appearance was spoiled only by foolish red wobbly flaps of skin protruding from their heads and necks. These odd protuberances would be unsightly whether the birds were alive or dead, but, as Giles was quick to suggest, the royal cooks could easily cover them up with a strategic pastry ruff or a cunningly fashioned collar of cabbage leaves.

The big birds' conversation was less alluring than the chickens' gentle clucking. As the huntsmen wove in and out among them, trying to scoop up a bird in their arms, the turkeys' harsh, throaty cackle became more raucous by the minute. Undeterred by these sound effects, Giles soon managed to corner a healthy-looking specimen against the garden wall. While Giles bent towards it with arms outstretched, making what he hoped was an enticing "chook, chook, chook!" noise, Piers leapt behind the fat creature and shooed it towards his friend. A little closer… and up! Gratefully, Giles flung his arms around the shock of white feathers, pinned its wings to its sides, and swept the big bird off its feet.

"Ha!" he cried. "That wasn't so hard. Now we've just got to get it back to the palace."

"I hope the Queen will like it," said Giles as they headed back through the forest. He was not looking forward to the Queen's reaction to those hideous red flaps.

With a flash of inspiration, Piers extracted a small, dark woollen hood from the leather pouch that hung from his belt. He'd been using it the day before when hunting with one of the royal falcons. The hood was a tight fit for the less streamlined turkey, but it was soon secured over its head. The turkey immediately fell silent, as subdued as if night had just fallen.

"I expect the Queen will like it once she's tasted it," Piers said hopefully. "There'll certainly be plenty of flesh to go round."

Conscious that the daylight was now fading fast, the huntsmen walked briskly, discussing how each would spend his share of the ten guineas reward. The bird grew heavier by the minute. As they neared the forest's boundary, they passed a familiar hollow tree, often cited as a landmark for navigation due to a distinctive large hole in the trunk at shoulder height.

"Just a moment!" cried Piers. "I think there's someone watching us from inside the hole in the hollow tree. Halt! Who goes there? Someone else trying to win the Queen's Christmas favour, I'll be bound. Well, I'm not having it! Giles, hide that turkey while I take a look."

Giles raised his eyebrows, wondering exactly where he was meant to conceal a bird the size of a small child.

Piers rushed forward, adrenalin pumping in anticipation of challenging a rival. He thrust both arms inside the hole, expecting to grasp the varmint's neck. His attack was met not with human cries but with a startled avian squawk. Hastily withdrawing his hands, he found he was clutching not the neck of another huntsman but the body of a large owl, soft, white, and fluffy as snow. The bird blinked one startled amber eye at him and strained its wings against Piers' cupped palms, clearly optimistic that it might escape.

Giles let out a cry of admiration. "I say, Piers, that's a beauty! Do you think we should take it back as another suggestion for the Queen's Christmas dinner? There's nothing unsightly about that specimen!"

Piers straightened his arms so that he could admire the bird at a greater distance.

"By George, I think we should," he agreed. "It's certainly a handsome fellow. Not sure how much flesh it has on it" - gently he squeezed the lightweight body - "but it would certainly look a treat on a silver platter."

To keep its broad wings under control, Piers tucked the bird close against his chest. Its tiny heart fluttered undetected through the huntsman's leather jerkin. It was a comfortable arrangement for them both.

Once back at the castle, the two huntsmen sought permission of the Queen's lady in waiting to show their catch to their mistress. They were soon admitted to the royal bedchamber where the Queen was still toying listlessly with her embroidery.

Giles set the turkey gently down on the floor at his feet, its head and neck still concealed by the woollen hood. The big, ungainly bird took a few unsteady steps, trying to acclimatize to the hard, chilly flagstones that felt so different from the soft floor of the walled garden. Stumbling across a discarded croquet mallet, it took comfort in settling on the handle, wrapping its long claws securely around the wooden shaft. With the emission of a contented "caw", it appeared to have settled down to roost.

The Queen looked at the turkey thoughtfully.

"Nice white feathers," she appraised. "They'd make a pretty decoration for my hair on Christmas Day. Plenty of meat on it too."

She approached the roosting bird and reached out to prod its back with the end of her golden embroidery scissors. It didn't flinch. Then she turned to inspect the smaller, fluffier bundle that the second huntsman was clutching to his chest.

"What have you got there, Piers?" she questioned.

Piers gently set the fragile creature down on the floor. Appreciating the warmth of the candlelit room, the owl turned its head around slowly, taking in its new surroundings. Sidestepping a few paces, it stared hard for a moment at its captor. Then it paced over to inspect the turkey, which was by now emitting a low, steady rumble that sounded remarkably like a human snore. The owl looked at the turkey, then at the Queen, who was silently engrossed in assessing how much meat might be concealed under that feathery wrapper. While the Queen was busy wondering whether she could eat the whole thing herself, the owl slowly made its way towards her and stood quietly for a moment at her feet, contemplating its next action.

And then it decided. With a rattling, hacking cough it opened its beak and expelled a dark brown furry pellet that landed neatly on the lacy hem of the Queen's long ivory silken gown.

"Ugh! What on earth is THAT?" spluttered the Queen, teetering backwards and shaking her skirts anxiously. "The wretched thing's attacking me!"

Giles stepped forward and bent to inspect the owl's emission. "It appears to be dried matted fur, blood, and – yes, a few bone fragments too, Your Majesty," he reported. He bowed courteously, as if he'd just paid her a compliment. "I believe that's how owls expel their digestive waste. It's the remains of a mouse or a rat that it had for lunch."

The Queen shuddered. "Surely you don't expect me to eat something that's got THAT muck inside it?" she shrieked.

The owl, which had been looking rather pleased with its performance, spread its snowy wings and fluttered silently up to perch on a brass candelabra, which scarcely stirred beneath the bird's barely perceptible weight. Giles, meanwhile, had turned his attention to the larger bird, which was still perched contentedly on the croquet mallet. He extended his arm in its direction, as if offering a formal introduction.

"Then might I suggest the turkey, Your Majesty?"

The Queen nodded quickly, anxious to conclude the matter so that she could change into a fresh gown.

"Yes, yes, we'll have the turkey. Now take them both away."

She rang the bell for her wardrobe mistress and swept from the room, leaving Piers to coax the owl down from the candelabra. Meanwhile Giles hoisted the huge turkey into his arms to escort it to the kitchen.

As the huntsmen headed down the spiral staircase bearing both birds, they encountered Maria, Giles's ladylove, rushing to respond to the Queen's summons. She'd heard of their mission and was eager to learn the outcome. While Giles explained, Piers mischievously whisked the woollen hood off the turkey's head. He hoped to frighten Maria with its ugly red wattles, causing her to faint into his friend's arms.

"Ugh! Why on earth did Her Majesty choose that hideous creature instead of this gorgeous little owl?" she questioned, stroking the docile bird on the top of its head and wondering what it would taste like braised in mead. Assuming it was no longer under threat of execution, the owl happily allowed her this liberty.

"Oh, there's nothing really surprising about that," said Giles. "The problem is that turkey doesn't have its own defence missile system."

The End

Thank You for Reading These Stories

If you enjoyed them, you might also like to read Debbie Young's *Stocking Fillers*, a collection of twelve short stories for the Christmas season, now available to buy in paperback and ebook editions from all good retailers.

To find out more about Debbie Young's fiction, and to be among the first to know about new titles, visit her website: www.authordebbieyoung.com or follow her on Twitter at @DebbieYoungBN.

Printed in Great Britain
by Amazon